Snowbound

by Kiki Thorpe

illustrated by Mel Grant

SCHOLASTIC INC.

New York Toronto London Auckland Sydney
Mexico City New Delhi Hong Kong

Based on the TV series *The Wild Thornberrys*® created by Klasky Csupo, Inc.
as seen on Nickelodeon®

ISBN 0-439-24180-4

12 11 10 9 8 7 6 5 4 3 2 1   1 2 3 4 5 6/0

Printed in the U.S.A.
First Scholastic printing, February 2001

Discovery Facts

Snow leopards live high in the Himalayan (Hi-mah-LAY-an) Mountains in Central Asia. They have heavy fur on the bottoms of their paws to protect them from snow and ice. When it's very cold, snow leopards keep their noses warm by holding the ends of their long, furry tails in their mouths.

Although there are laws to protect them, snow leopards are often hunted for their beautiful fur. They are an endangered species.

"Come out and play, Darwin!" Eliza cried.
She packed a snowball and tossed it to
Darwin.

"I'm fine here," Darwin sniffed.
"Chimpanzees were not meant to play in the
snow."

The Thornberrys had come to the
Himalayan Mountains to film the wild
yaks that lived there. But while they
were there, Eliza had a plan of her
own. She was going to meet a
snow leopard.

"Lunchtime!" Marianne called.

"Yum! Hot chocolate!" Eliza exclaimed.

"Actually, it's a kind of local tea," Marianne told her. "It's made with yak butter."

"Ugh," Debbie said. "Why can't I have soda like a normal teenager? May I be excused?"

"Actually, I'd like to be excused too," Eliza said. "I'm going to try to find a snow leopard."

"You won't see a snow leopard around here. They are rare, lonely creatures, and hardly ever seen," Nigel told her.

"Eliza, it's very cold out there,"
Marianne warned. "These mountains can
be dangerous if you aren't prepared."

"Don't worry, Mom," Eliza said. "I'll be
careful." She put on a big coat, mittens, and a
warm hat. Then she put her compass in her
pocket. "Let's go, Darwin!"

Darwin followed her outside. "Gee, Eliza,
do you think this is a good idea?" he asked.

"Oh, Darwin. We'll be fine. Come on!
I want to find the snow leopard before
it gets dark."

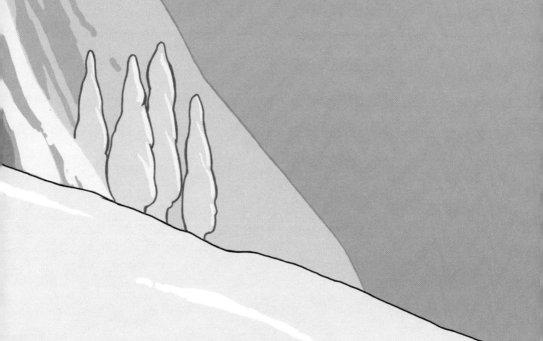

"Now, if you were a snow leopard, where would you be?" Eliza asked Darwin.

"I'd be inside drinking hot tea," Darwin answered.

"I'll bet a snow leopard might live in those rocks over there," Eliza said. She pointed at a pile of rocks. They looked very far away to Darwin.

"I think I'll stay here," he told Eliza.

"Suit yourself," she said. She started walking through the snow.

Just then a yak sneezed—Ah-CHOOOO! It frightened Darwin.

"Wait, Eliza!" he cried. "I'm coming too!"

Eliza and Darwin walked for a long time.

"We're going too far," Darwin complained. "We're going to get lost."

"We're not going to get lost," Eliza told him. "We can follow our tracks back home. Besides, I brought my compass. I know exactly where we are going."

"Chimpanzees shouldn't be walking through the snow looking for leopards." Darwin shivered.

"Darwin, this might be our only chance to ever see a snow leopard," Eliza said. "Let's go a little farther."

At last they reached the rocks. But there was no snow leopard.

"Too bad," said Darwin. "Let's go home."

"Just a little longer, Darwin," Eliza said sadly. She had been sure they would find a snow leopard.

As Eliza walked around the rocks, Darwin sat down to rest. Suddenly he smelled something *delicious*! It smelled like food cooking!

Darwin followed the scent over a hill and saw . . . the Commvee! Eliza and Darwin had been walking in a circle!

"Eliza, look! We're home!" Darwin cried as he hurried toward the van. But the wind carried Darwin's voice away. Eliza didn't hear him.

In the Commvee, Marianne was cooking dinner. Darwin felt warm and cozy after his long walk. Soon he was fast asleep.

"I didn't see anything over there, Darwin," Eliza said as she came back around the rocks. But Darwin wasn't there.

"Darwin!" she called. "Darwin, where are you?" There was no answer.

"Where could he be?" Eliza asked herself. "It's starting to snow. We need to go home."

Suddenly she saw footprints in the snow. Eliza gasped. They looked like the paw prints of a leopard! Could the snow leopard have gotten Darwin?

Eliza was worried. "Darwin!" she cried again.

As Eliza looked for Darwin, the falling snow turned into a blizzard!

Soon Eliza's tracks were covered in snow. "I'm glad I brought my compass," she said. She reached into her pocket for it—but the compass was gone!

"Oh, no!" she cried.

Eliza had to find Darwin, and she had to find her way home. "Darwin! Darwin! Darwin!" Eliza called.

"Eliza! Eliza! Eliza!" called Eliza's family. They were very worried. Darwin was worried too. He thought that Eliza had come home with him. But now she was lost in the snow!

Eliza didn't even want to meet the snow leopard anymore. She just wanted to find Darwin and go home.

"I never should have made Darwin come with me," she said to herself. "He was right. A chimpanzee doesn't belong in the snow."

Eliza peered into the blizzard. Something was coming toward her!

"It's Darwin!" she exclaimed. But wait! It was much too big to be Darwin. Eliza watched as the creature came closer and closer. . . .

Suddenly Eliza found herself face to face with a snow leopard!

"Don't be afraid," the snow leopard purred.

"My friend Darwin is lost!" Eliza cried. "Have you seen him?"

"Your friend is safe," the snow leopard told her. "I saw him go back to the moving cave you live in."

"You mean the Commvee?" Eliza asked. "Can you help me get there?"

The snow leopard paused. "Okay. But we should hurry. This storm will get worse before it gets better," she said. "Follow me."

Eliza was so excited to be talking to the snow leopard that she almost forgot about the blizzard.

"What's your name?" she asked. "Where do you come from?"

"My name is Singa. These mountains are my home," the leopard answered.

Eliza was about to ask another question, when she heard a noise.

"Eliza!" the voice called.

"That sounds like Debbie," Eliza said. "I wonder what she's doing out in this storm."

Before she knew it, Eliza found herself back at the Commvee.

"I'm home! And there's Darwin!" she exclaimed. "Thank you, Singa!" She turned to say good-bye to her new friend, but Singa was gone.

"Eliza! You're safe!" Eliza's parents cried.

"Guess what!" Eliza said. "I met a snow leopard!"

"I think all this cold has frozen your brain," Debbie told her.

"Come on, everyone," Marianne said. "Let's get inside and warm up."

Inside, Eliza gave Darwin a big hug.

"I'm glad I found you, Darwin," Eliza said.

"I'm glad to be found," said Darwin,
hugging his friend.